FLAT STANLEY
On Ice

EGMONT

We bring stories to life

Book Band: Green

First published in Great Britain 2017
This Reading Ladder edition published 2017
by Egmont UK Limited
The Yellow Building, 1 Nicholas Road, London W11 4AN
Text copyright © 2015 by the Trust u/w/o Richard C. Brown a/k/a Jeff Brown f/b/o Duncan Brown
Illustrations copyright © 2017 by the Trust u/w/o Richard C. Brown a/k/a Jeff Brown
f/b/o Duncan Brown
ISBN 978 1 4052 8354 0
www.egmont.co.uk
A CIP catalogue record for this title is available from the British Library.
Printed in Singapore
63263/1

Series consultant: Nikki Gamble

MIX
Paper
FSC FSC® C018306

FLAT STANLEY

On Ice

Written by Lori Haskins Houran   Illustrations by Jon Mitchell

Based on the original character created by Jeff Brown

Reading Ladder

Stanley Lambchop lived with his mother, his father, and his little brother, Arthur.

Stanley was four feet tall, about a foot wide and half an inch thick.

He had been flat ever since a bulletin board fell on him.

Stanley was still discovering new things about being flat.

It turned out he was great at catching snowflakes!

Stanley was not so good at making snow angels.

'You're too flat to sink into the snow!'
said Arthur.

'Never mind,' said Stanley. 'Let's just
go to the skating pond.'
They saw lots of people they knew out
skating.

'Hi, Arthur! Hi, Stanley!' called their
friend Martin Tibbs.

Their sports teacher, Coach Bart,
waved hello.

'I can't wait to get on the ice!' said Arthur, grabbing his skates.

Now that Stanley's feet were flat, they didn't fit into skates any more.

But Stanley wondered if he could just use his feet as skates!

'I hope this works,' he said.

Stanley stood up on the ice.

He pushed off with his left foot, then his right.

16

Stanley couldn't believe how terrific he
was at skating.

It was his best flat discovery yet!

'Look at his spin!' said Martin.

'Did he just carve his name in the ice?' gasped Coach Bart.

'I can make a snow angel,' said Arthur.

Stanley swooped and glided for hours.

Arthur skated, too, but he did more sliding than gliding.

'Phew! I'm hot,' said Arthur after a while. He took off his jacket.
'Me too,' said Martin.

23

They weren't the only ones who felt it getting warmer.

Coach Bart blew his whistle.

'Everyone off the ice!'

'Noooooo!' complained the skaters.

'I brought hot chocolate!' he said.

In six seconds, the ice was empty.

Except for Stanley. He was still skating in the middle of the pond.

'STAN-LEY!' yelled Arthur.

'STAN-LEY!' yelled Martin.

Out on the ice, Stanley heard his name. 'Wow,' he said. 'They're cheering! I'd better put on a good show.'

Stanley sped up. He pushed off hard using his big toe and did the splits in the air!

When he landed, there was a loud POP.

Stanley looked down.

The ice was cracking . . . right between his feet!

'Help!' cried Stanley. 'HELP!'

Arthur shouted back at him. 'LIE DOWN, STANLEY! MAKE A SNOW ANGEL!'

'Huh?' thought Stanley, confused.
Was this really the time to tease him
about snow angels?

So what if he was too flat to sink into
the snow?

Then Stanley understood.

If he lay down on the ice, he would
be too flat to sink!

Carefully, Stanley spread out.

He was safe for now.

But how could he get off the ice?

Back on shore, Arthur was busy.

'We need a rope!' he called. 'Help me
tie the scarves together. The arms of
the jackets, too!'

'Good thinking, Arthur,' said Coach Bart.

'We'll help!' said Martin.

All of the skaters pitched in. Soon they had a long rope to toss to Stanley.

Stanley caught it on the first try.

'PULL!' ordered Arthur.

Everyone gave a mighty tug.

Stanley came flying across the ice!

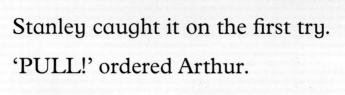

Stanley flew a little too well . . .

off the ice, past the skaters and

straight into a snow bank!

'I'm OK!' said Stanley, spitting out a
mouthful of snow.

Coach Bart poured hot chocolate for everyone. He raised his mug.

'Here's to Arthur Lambchop, who kept his cool when things got warm!' he said.

'Yay, Arthur!' everyone cheered.

Stanley cheered loudest of all.

And the next time the pond froze, Stanley gave Arthur an extra-big thanks.